The First Song Ever Sung

BY LAURA KRAUSS MELMED

ILLUSTRATED BY ED YOUNG

PUFFIN BOOKS

PUFFIN BOOKS
Published by the Penguin Group
Penguin Books USA Inc., 375 Hudson Street, New York, New York 10014, U.S.A.
Penguin Books Ltd, 27 Wrights Lane, London W8 5TZ, England
Penguin Books Australia Ltd, Ringwood, Victoria, Australia
Penguin Books Canada Ltd, 10 Alcorn Avenue, Toronto, Ontario, Canada M4V 3B2
Penguin Books (N.Z.) Ltd, 182-190 Wairau Road, Auckland 10, New Zealand

Penguin Books Ltd, Registered Offices: Harmondsworth, Middlesex, England

First published in the United States of America by Lothrop, Lee,
and Shepard Books, a division of William Morrow & Company, Inc., 1993
Reprinted by arrangement with William Morrow & Company, Inc.
Published in Puffin Books, 1995

1 3 5 7 9 10 8 6 4 2

Text copyright © Laura Krauss Melmed, 1993
Illustrations copyright © Ed Young, 1993
All rights reserved

LIBRARY OF CONGRESS CATALOGING-IN-PUBLICATION DATA
Melmed, Laura Krauss.
The first song ever sung / by Laura Krauss Melmed ; illustrated by Ed Young.
p.   cm. — (A picture Puffin book)
Summary: Animal and human friends provide lyrical answers to a young boy's musical query.
ISBN 0-14-055457-2
[1. Songs—Fiction. 2. Bedtime—Fiction.] I. Young, Ed, ill. II. Title. III. Series.
PZ7.M51627Fi   1995   [E]—dc20   94-44591   CIP   AC

Printed in the United States of America

to Jonathan, who asked the question

—LKM

to "the gardeners of the spirit who know that without darkness
nothing comes to birth as without light nothing flowers" — (ANON)

—EY

"What was the first song ever sung?"
said the little boy to his father.

"The first song ever sung was a strong song,
a man's song, a warrior's song, a friend's song,"
said the father to the little boy.

"What was the first song ever sung?"
said the little boy to his brother.

"The first song ever sung was a proud song,
a loud song, a stomping, shaking, shout song,"
said the brother to the little boy.

"What was the first song ever sung?"
said the little boy to his sister.

"The first song ever sung was a rope song,
a swing song, a jumping, twirling, leap song,"
said the sister to the little boy.

"What was the first song ever sung?"
said the little boy to his grandmother.

"The first song ever sung was a spinning song,
a weaving song, a magic thread and thimble song,"
said the grandmother to the little boy.

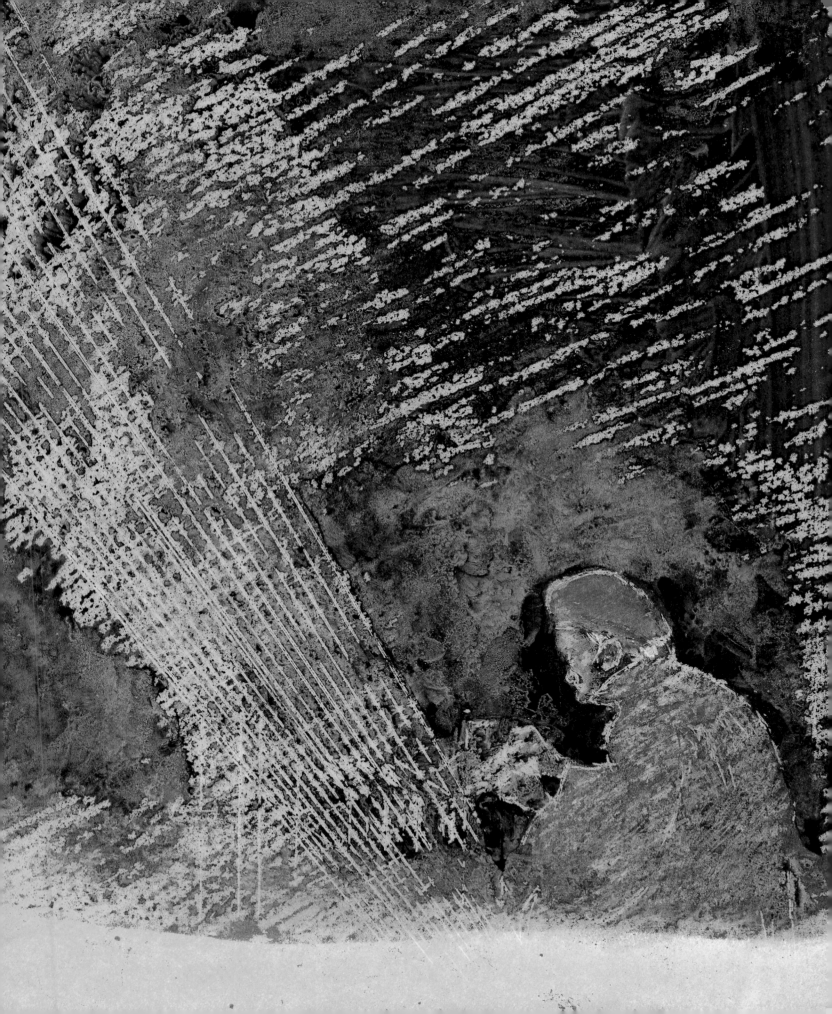

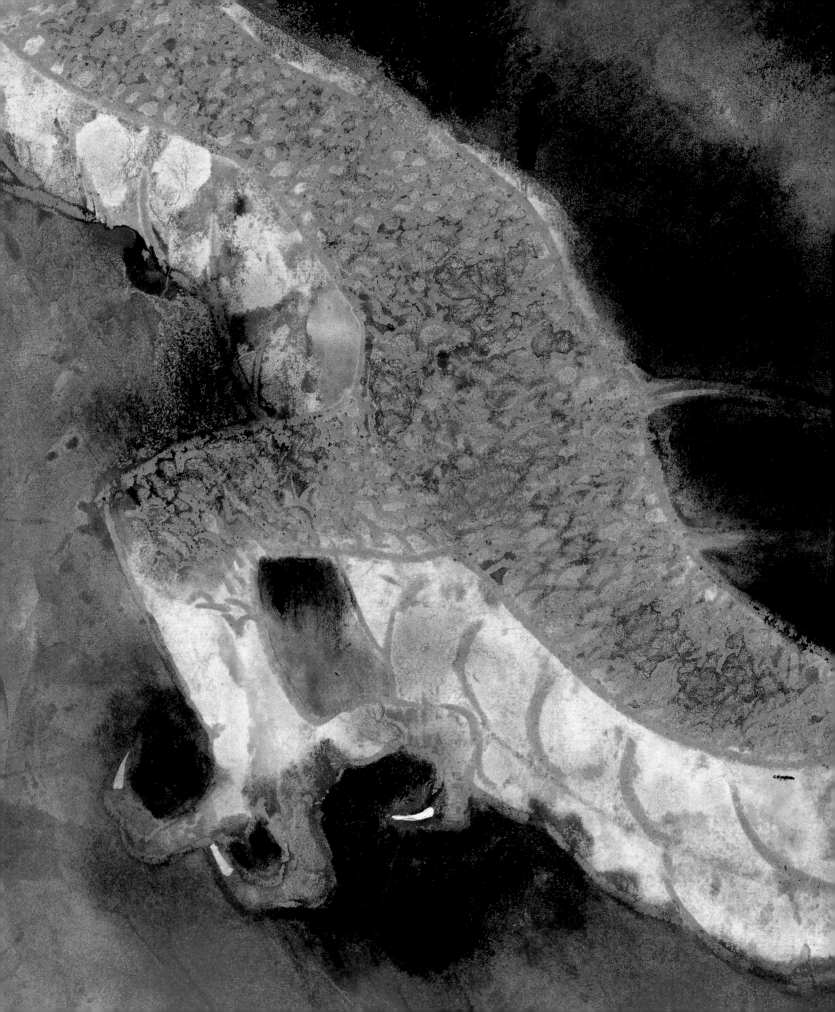

"What was the first song ever sung?"
said the little boy to his grandfather.

"The first song ever sung was a seed song,
a sprout song, a rain song, a harvest song,"
said the grandfather to the little boy.

"What was the first song ever sung?"
said the little boy to his dog.

"The first song ever sung was a moon song,
a howl song, a lone song, a bone song,"
said the dog to the little boy.

"What was the first song ever sung?"
said the little boy to the minnows in the brook.

"The first song ever sung was a ripple song,
a splash song, a pebble song, a flash song,"
said the minnows to the little boy.

"What was the first song ever sung?"
said the little boy to the birds in the sky.

"The first song ever sung was a sing song,
a wing song, a dawn song, a dream song,"
said the birds to the little boy.

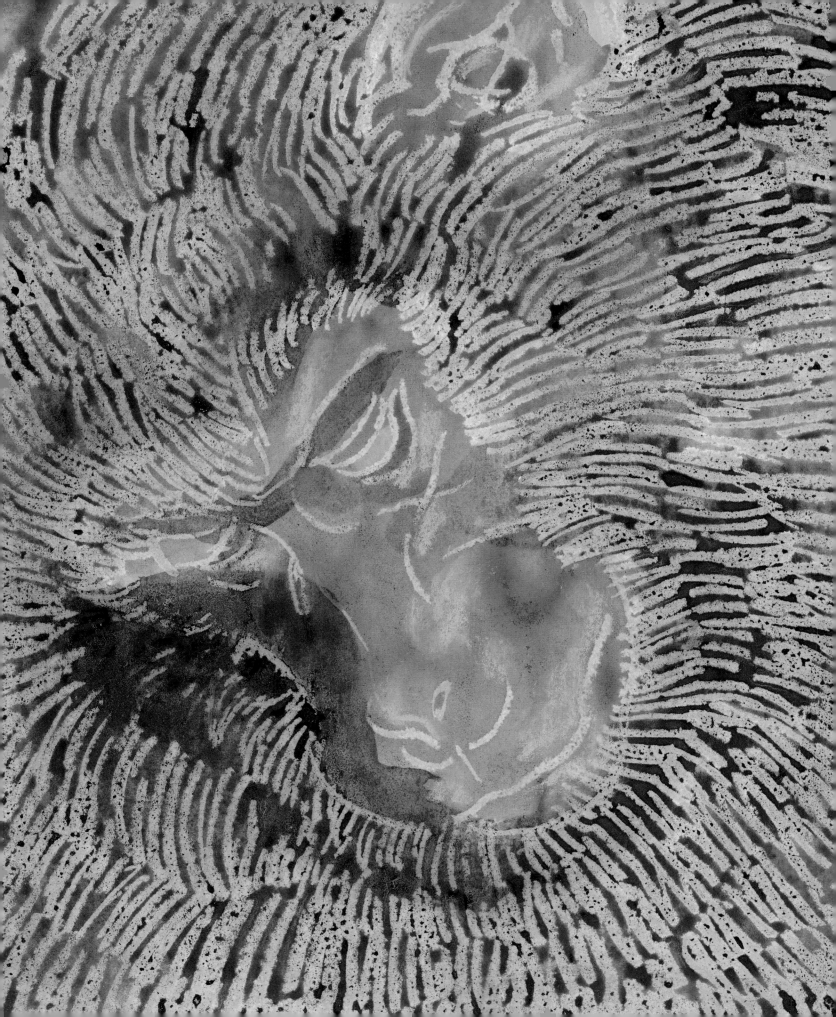

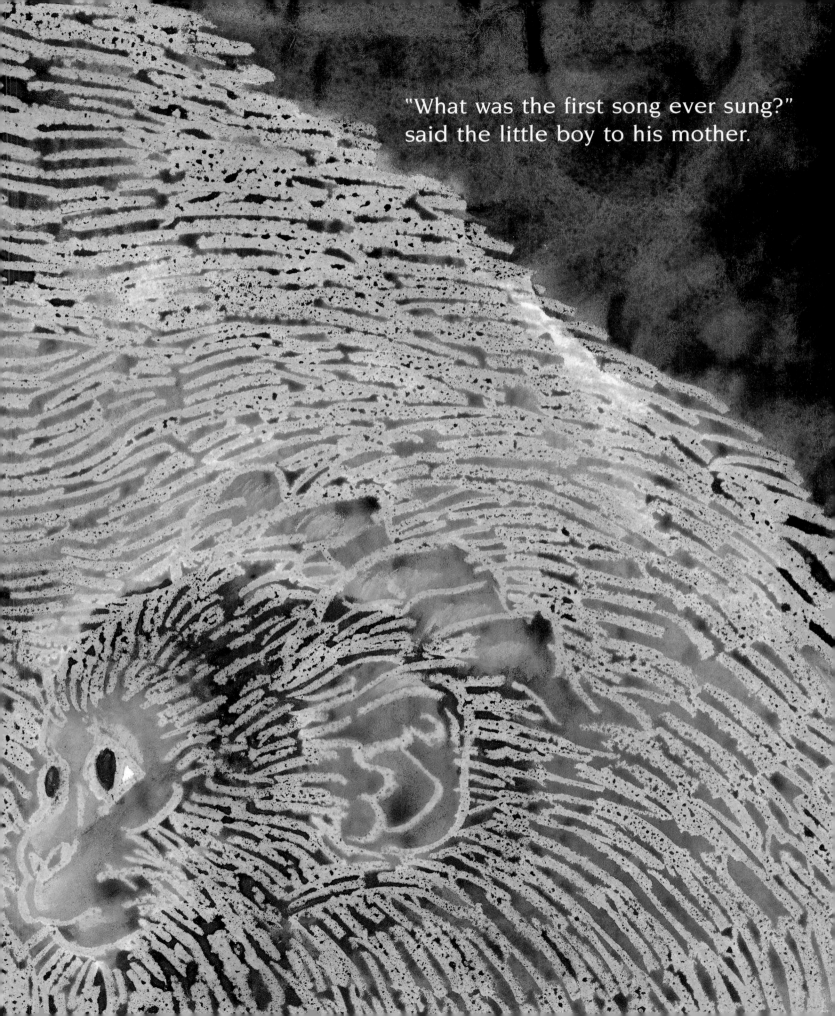

"What was the first song ever sung?"
said the little boy to his mother.

"The first song ever sung was a mother's song,
a hush song, a sleep song, a love song,"
said the mother to the little boy
as he climbed into her lap.

And she sang him gently to sleep.